111

Brave Charlotte

and the Wolves

For Vilma, anytime —A. S.

For Barbara, Claudia, Eva, Friederike, Gudrun, Julia,
Nureni, and Petra, and all other courageous women of
all shapes and sizes —H. W.

Text copyright © 2009 by Anu Stohner
Illustrations copyright © 2009 by Henrike Wilson

First published as *Charlotte und die Wölfe* in 2009
by Carl Hanser Verlag GmbH & Co KG, Germany
Published in the United States in 2009 by Bloomsbury U.S.A. Children's Books
175 Fifth Avenue, New York, New York 10010

Library of Congress Cataloging-in-Publication Data
Stohner, Anu.
[Charlotte und die Wölfe. English]
Brave Charlotte and the wolves / by Anu Stohner ; illustrated by Henrike Wilson.—1st U.S. ed.
p.   cm.
Summary: Charlotte the sheep proves her courage once again when the rest of her flock, including Wolfie and
his gang of pretend wolves, trembles in fear at the sound of howling in the forest.
ISBN-13: 978-1-59990-424-5 • ISBN-10: 1-59990-424-1 (hardcover)
ISBN-13: 978-1-59990-425-2 • ISBN-10: 1-59990-425-X (reinforced)
[1. Sheep—Fiction. 2. Courage—Fiction. 3. Gangs—Fiction. 4. Wolves—Fiction.]
I. Wilson, Henrike, ill. II. Title.
PZ7.S8699Brf 2009   [E]—dc22   2009007696

Typeset in Sabon
Art created with acrylics on cardboard

First U.S. Edition 2009
Printed in China by SNP Leefung Printers Limited
1 3 5 7 9 10 8 6 4 2 (hardcover)
1 3 5 7 9 10 8 6 4 2 (reinforced)

Brave Charlotte
and the Wolves

by Anu Stohner

illustrated by Henrike Wilson

BLOOMSBURY

NEW YORK BERLIN LONDON

Charlotte had always been different from the other sheep. She climbed trees and swam in the wild brook, and sometimes she even ran up the steep, sharp rocks where no sheep had ever been before. From there she could look far off into the distance, all the way to the wide and dangerous road.

Ever since Charlotte had helped save the old shepherd when he broke his leg, the older sheep had stopped worrying about her wild ways. The whole herd was proud of her—although they still didn't like watching her climb up high.

But when the older sheep praised Charlotte, there was a group of young sheep who rolled their eyes. "*Baaaa*, who cares?" they said, when no one was listening. "What's so brave about her?"

Their leader, a young sheep named Wolfie, said, "The next time something happens, *we'll* take charge."

Every morning, the group of young sheep would gather away
from the herd and Wolfie would ask, "What's our name?"

"The Wolves!" the others would answer in chorus.

"Who are we?" asked Wolfie.

"A big, bad gang!" they cried.

The Wolves liked to pick on Jack, the old sheepdog. They would
hide in the bushes so he'd think they had gone missing.

At night, when it was totally quiet, Wolfie and his gang would pretend to be real wolves. "*Ah-ooo, woo-woo-wooooo!*" they would howl. The little ones in the herd would run shaking back to their mothers, while Wolfie and his gang laughed.

Then one night, under a full moon, a real wolf's howl rang out from the forest. At first, it was so quiet it could have been the wind rustling the treetops. But the older sheep pricked up their ears.

"*Ah-ooo, woo-woo-wooooo!*" This time the howl was much louder and more frightening.

"Wolves!" whispered the sheep.

All night the sheep huddled together, and when morning came, they could still hear the wolves: "*Ah-ooo, woo-woo-wooooo!*"

"Someone must do something!" said one of the sheep. "The shepherd must send Jack to scare them away."

"Jack? But he's even afraid of Wolfie and his friends."

The sheep shook their heads. Who was going to help them?

"I'll go and take a look," said Charlotte.

The others were very nervous. "A sheep going to check on wolves? Unheard of!" But Charlotte could not hear them. She was already on her way.

And Wolfie and his gang—where were they?

Quietly, quietly, Charlotte tiptoed through the forest. She didn't see any wolves, but from time to time she could hear the howling—and it was getting louder. "*Ah-ooo, woo-woo-wooooo!*"

Quietly, quietly, Charlotte tiptoed over to the wild brook. But there was no trace of the wolves. Charlotte took a drink, then decided she needed a better view.

Quietly, quietly, Charlotte tiptoed up the sharp rocks. She pricked up her ears, but everything was silent. Then she heard the howl once more, "*Ah-ooo, woo-woo-wooooo!*" It was very close by—and it came from above!

Suddenly Charlotte knew how the other sheep felt when they watched her climbing up high. She didn't want to look up! When she finally did, she didn't see any wolves. Not a single one. There, high up on the rocks . . .

. . . was a scruffy little puppy! It howled so loudly that Charlotte's curly sheep hair bristled. The puppy was stuck all alone up there. Charlotte rushed to help.

"Where did you get such a scary voice?" Charlotte asked when they arrived at the foot of the hill together.

"Everyone in my family has it," sniffled the puppy. "It's probably because my great-grandfather was a wolf."

The puppy's name was Mimi. She had been traveling on the big road with her humans, she explained, and they had stopped for a picnic. Mimi had gone exploring in the forest when suddenly it became dark and she got lost. "*Ah-ooo, woo-woo-wooooo!*" she howled again.

"Okay, okay," said Charlotte. "I'll take you back to the picnic area." But first, Charlotte had a plan, and as soon as Mimi heard it, she began to howl again—this time with glee.

When Charlotte trotted out of the forest a little while later, the whole herd was happy to see her return. "She's done it!" said the sheep. "We can't hear the wolves anymore! She's chased them away."

But just then a howl rang out, louder than ever: "*Ah-ooo, woo-woo-wooooo!*" The herd stood frozen with fear.

So why was Charlotte smiling?

"Don't be afraid!" she said. "They won't hurt us. They're waiting in the forest."

"What are they waiting *for*?" asked the sheep with shaking voices.

"To meet *our* Wolves," Charlotte said. "I explained to them that we have wolves of our own, and they would like to meet them."

The older sheep nodded in understanding and called out for Wolfie. But Wolfie and his gang were crouched behind the bushes, hoping that no one could see them.

"I'll tell them that our Wolves don't have time today," said Charlotte with a smile. "Perhaps they can visit another time."

Once Charlotte went back into the forest, Wolfie and his friends came out from their hiding place. "Didn't you hear us calling you?" asked the older sheep.

"Us? No," said Wolfie. "We didn't hear anything."

"Not one sheep in your whole gang?" asked the older sheep.

"What gang?" Wolfie asked his friends. "Have you ever heard anything about a gang?"

Exactly at that moment a howl rang out from the forest. It sounded as if the wolf was also laughing: "*Ah-ooo, ha-ha-ha-wooooo!*" Wolfie and his friends ran like lightning back into the bushes.

The older sheep only laughed: "*Baa-ha-ha, baa-ha-ha!*"

And Charlotte? As promised, she took Mimi to the picnic area by the road, where the humans wrapped their arms around their puppy. They had searched for her the entire night. Mimi howled once more with glee. "*Ah-ooo, woo-woo-wooooo!*" Charlotte smiled, knowing that "the Wolves" could hear—and they were probably hiding in the bushes.

If you enjoyed this story, read another great
adventure featuring one very special little sheep . . .

BRAVE
Charlotte

Anu Stohner · Henrike Wilson

A New York Times Best Illustrated Book